Stav enjoys playing sports and wrote her first book on similar challenges that she has faced whilst growing up as a girl who strayed from social norms and played football. She hopes that her book helps to breakdown stereotypes and encourages everybody to challenge social norms.

WHY CAN'T YOU JUST BE A NORMAL *Girl?*

By Stav Williams

AUSTIN MACAULEY PUBLISHERS™
LONDON • CAMBRIDGE • NEW YORK • SHARJAH

Copyright © Stav Williams (2020)

A CIP catalogue record for this title is available from the British Library.

ISBN 9781528984522 (Paperback)
ISBN 9781528984539 (ePub e-book)

www.austinmacauley.com

First Published (2020)
Austin Macauley Publishers Ltd
25 Canada Square
Canary Wharf
London
E14 5LQ

I would like to thank everyone at Austin Macauley Publishers for this opportunity, as well as the fantastic support and work with the publication of this book.

I would like to acknowledge my family and friends, thank you all for your consistent and boundless support, joy and love.

Dear Mum,

I thank you every day for every single one of your sacrifices, and I remain eternally grateful for all that you have given me. Here's to you – the strongest, kindest, smartest, most incredible person I know. Thanks for always believing in me.

Table of Contents

Ready, Set, Normal

The mirror on my bedroom wall begins to fog up as I breathe heavily, staring closely at my reflection. My hands make their way around my face, pinching and prodding the excess skin. And, my eyebrows raise up and down as I continue to ask myself that one important, mind boggling, overused, over exerted, never-ending question. That continues to hang over my head like the chimpanzees at the zoo that hang off the branches, to which, they too, ask me that one important question, that is: "WHY CAN'T YOU JUST BE A NORMAL GIRL?"

It seemed clear to me that there was something about how I am or who I am that didn't fit. That wasn't recognisable with the people I knew. That made me different to everybody else, every other girl. Something that caught the eyes of everyone that stared at me every time I entered the room and watched with anticipation, as if they were relying on my every move. Something that entertained the laughter behind my back that grew louder and louder, to explode through the drums of my ears. Something that provoked the pushes and the shoves down the long winding corridors, that seemed to have escaped the sight of everyone responsible enough to stop them. And something that would spark the comments, the over exhausted comments, that bounced around the playground quicker than the balls I kicked, and threw, and hit. Each, to the same old tune.

Whatever it was about me that made me stand out, must've been a bad thing. Certainly, a bad thing to be, right?

So, what was it? What wasn't so normal about me? What was it that made this question so known to everybody else?

And, how could I fix it?

Because perhaps fixing it would make me feel as though I belong, as though I was comfortable, as though I was free… If I listen to what they say and change it, then maybe, just maybe, I'd be normal. I'd be the normal girl they talk about.

And as I stare in the mirror, in the way, speaks the words they always say: "Why can't you just be a normal girl?"

Well, if that's what you want me to be...

I'll listen to you,

I'll take it in,

I'll change it up, I'll change within,

Until 'normal', describes me.

A Dress to Impress

"ALISON, ARE YOU READY YET?!" My great aunt Cecilia yells as she bursts her way through the hallway and into my bedroom. By which time, her jaw had dropped extremely low, lower than it had ever been before. Even lower than the time I kicked a ball towards the house. Which, not only managed to slice the heads off her precious, "well regarded" tulips, but shattered through the top righthand corner of the sitting room window. Yikes! What had I done this time?

My heart began to race as I awaited, in fear, of what was to come. Before I could find the words to ask her what was wrong, she continued in great rage: "WHAT ARE YOU WEARING?!" Slightly puzzled and misdirected, I looked down to explore what was so bad about my choice of clothes. What did she mean? What was she so angry about?

I replied with an "Erm" and thankfully, after a few painful seconds, she saved me from the confusion, and impatiently explained:

"You can't be in shorts and your hair is a mess!

Where is your gown? You need to impress.

We are going to a ball. You cannot go like that.

The whole town will be there, from the reception and back.

All the girls will be in dresses, every single one.

Why can't you be like them? You'll have far more fun.

Why can't you just be a normal girl, Alison? Come on, don't frown.

We'll tidy you up, we'll find that gown."

Within seconds aunt Cecilia launched herself into my wardrobe. Remerging through the wall of clothes I had built to hide the hideousness of the dresses behind. I froze in silence. Aunt Cecilia wasn't usually this mad when I wore my clothes.

Although head shakes, rolled eyes, and multiple demands to get changed were common, this time she was really mad!

"Ah, there it is!" She pulled out the pink one, the long pink one, the most hideous long pink one - with the bits hanging off. "Now! put it on! Quickly! You've already made us late!"

To much of my disapproval, I began to take off my clothes. And as soon as they were off, she rushed to place it over my head.

And as it swayed down and drooped over my body, I looked down in disgust...Was this what I needed to do to impress?

What was so normal about this hideous dress?

Was it the frills? Was it the pink?

Was it the material? That really stinks!

Was it the sequins? Was it the bows?

The way is rested on my toes?

And this, this ridiculous pink dress,

Was the only way I could impress?

I wasn't happy, nor did she care, as she ran the brush through my hair. "Now, you put those nice shoes on and you'll be ok, and in a few minutes, we'll be on our way."

Shortly after, we arrived, and as the car drove up towards the drive, I caught a glimpse of the gardens that were occupied by the boys. Of course, they were all in shorts and were allowed to play outside! The car reached to a halt outside the grand entrance of the building, and every single part of me wanted to stay put, wanted to be anywhere else but here – in a dress. I already felt uncomfortable in what I was wearing, let alone wearing it in front of hundreds of people. Then, I remembered…this was my chance at being normal. This could help me fit in with them all. And that's what I needed, that's what was important. I counted down from ten and opened the door. I stumbled out of the car and sorted out some uncomfortable bits before proceeding to walk.

Aunt Cecilia hurried me along and lead me through to the hall.

She was right, all the girls were in dresses. I recognised Melissa, Poppy, Natalie and Emma from school. They all clumped together with their backs straight, noses pointed and their eyes drawing towards me – in unison.

Emma: "OMG is that Alison in a dress?"

Poppy: "LOL, well it's about time she did impress"

Within seconds I became the talk of the room. The noise levels increased, and crowds began to gather as if, for some miraculous reason, I became an attraction, luring them in, nourishing their curiosity, sparking their commentary:

Melissa: "Good job Alison, you look good, you dressed correctly, I hoped you would"

Poppy: "Now straighten your back and show us your grin, isn't it nice to just fit in"

Natalie: "That's a pretty dress, I have that one too. It's so lovely, it's so you"

"It's so you…It's so you…" I mumbled as I processed their thoughts… Is it so me?

I abandoned the conversations and bolted out of the hall, running through the hallway searching for an escape, searching for silence. I entered the last room at the bottom of the corridor, slammed the door behind me, and began to catch my breath.

As I recovered, I looked up and there I was staring back at me through the giant mirror that hung above the fireplace.

I walked slowly towards my reflection and in the way, spoke the words they always say:

"Why can't you just be a normal girl?"

Well, if that's what you want me to be;

I'll stop with the shorts, I'll tidy the 'mess',

I'll wear a gown and dress to impress,

But really, that's not me.

Girl + Ball + Mud + a Desire to Score a Goal = Ballet

It was Saturday. Saturday, Saturday, Saturday. The day I had been waiting for, to show what I can do once more. It was the day of the trials at the local football club. And it was my chance to prove that I could play too. I sprung out of bed and threw on my clothes, grabbed my boots and headed for the club.

The walk seemed longer than usual, maybe it was the excitement. I had been waiting, for what feels like forever, for this day. Sure, I played football every day afterschool at the park, but this day was special. This time I'll get to play with the boys. And I've been practising my shooting so hopefully I'll score, and when they're impressed, I'll play some more.

I eventually reached the club where a crowd of rowdy boys awaited instruction. As I approached the guys, little to my surprise, the giggles had started, the fingers pointed, and the comments harmonised as if they jointed:

"Who is she? What's her name? There's no place for a girl in this game!"

"What's she doing? Where's her skirt? She can't play with us in the dirt."

"RIGHT BOYS!" suddenly interrupted by the coach, the boys silently listened to the instructions: "SPLIT YOURSELVES INTO TWO TEAMS AND LET'S GET GOING. WE DON'T HAVE LONG."

The boys quickly organised themselves onto the pitch, and surprisingly seemed to have ignored that I was here. What was their problem? I'm here to play too, "she can't play" – Ha! I'll show you. I placed myself onto the nearest team and waited for the ball to come my way. Deep breaths in, deep breaths out, scoring that goal is what it's all about. The opposite team misplaced a pass and the ball came travelling towards me—I have the ball, what shall I do? I will go for it and run through. Keeping my rage in every turn, every move, every spin. Getting past one, two, three, those boys can't stop me. This is it, I'm going to shoot, right foot, I'll give it a good boot. Oh no, I fell. I'm lying there hoping I did well. No cheer, I hear, but up I get, and look at the goal with the ball in the net!

YES! I did it, I scored! The field immediately hushed, and the boys froze as they attended the coach's roar from the side-line: "EXCUSE ME MISS, LEAVE THEM ALONE, COLLECT YOUR THINGS AND HEAD ON HOME. THIS IS FOOTBALL, GIRLS DON'T PLAY, THEY TWIRL AROUND AND DO BALLET!"

Why is he saying that? Did he not see me score? Was that not enough? Did he want more? The field then broke into laughter at the expense of my confusion. And the louder that the sound of amusement echoed through my ears, the smaller and smaller I felt. "COME ON, YOU KNOW YOU DON'T BELONG HERE, WHY CAN'T YOU JUST BE A NORMAL GIRL M' DEAR?!"

Hurried by the coach, I bowed my head and withdrew myself from the field. Whilst trying to swallow the lump in the back of my throat, I grabbed my belongings and silently walked away. It was as if the world had crumbled on me, all at once. That everything I had been hoping for was suddenly taken away. And because of what? Because I was a girl?

I took the long route home, through town, hoping that my tears would dry out by the time I reached my front door. Aunt Cecilia wouldn't have understood the pain, in fact she would have probably told me off for going there in the first place! I didn't understand. How could something that makes me feel so happy, be so 'wrong'?

And why couldn't I play with the boys? It wasn't as if they were better than me, I was good enough to score!

My thoughts began to drown out to the sound of classical music that played along one of the side roads. Out of curiosity I wiped my tears and followed the noise that led me to the dance studio. I looked through the window and recognised the faces of some of the girls who were doing ballet inside. It was Melissa and the girls again! Melissa soon spotted me watching and ran to fetch me from outside. "Hi Alison! Are you here to join in? We'll show you the ropes and where to begin." Fuelled with excitement, Melissa grabbed my hand and dragged me into the room: "Hey girls! This is cray! Look who's come to do ballet."

"No way!!" The girls all ran towards me and welcomed me into the session. It was very overwhelming! I didn't really want to be in here but maybe I needed to. Maybe this is what I should have been doing! I don't think I had ever been in a dance studio before, I would have remembered the daunting mirrored walls and the echo of the floor boards. I noticed Natalie run off to her bag and pick out a tutu from her rather large collection. She ran back towards us and held it up against my waist.

The room squealed with. delight and issued directions:

Natalie: "Hold up this tutu and give us a twirl"

Poppy: "And do it gracefully, you know, like a girl!"

I didn't really 'know' what Poppy quite meant by this but supplying to the demand I gave them a twirl. And as I turned towards the mirror in the way, spoke the words they always say:

"Why can't you just be a normal girl?"

Well, if that's what you want me to be;

I'll stop with the football, and let the boys to play,

To twirl around and do ballet,

But really, that's not ME.

The Face Is a Canvas

"FIRST POSITION" Yells our ballet teacher, Sally, hurrying us to start. The sound of feet scurrying into place on the wooden floor of the dance studio became an all-too familiar sound on my Saturday mornings. That, and the smell of 'The All New Cherry-Max Lip Balm' that seemed to linger amongst the girls. As much as the physical demands of pointed toes, straightened back and muscle tension began to tidy up my movement, I still hadn't quite got the gist of it all. And I wasn't too decided on wanting to either! I hardly ever made it from first position to fifth without messing it up or stumbling over my feet.

The sluggish clock hands eventually reached noon as the class drew to an end. I usually ran off at this point, I didn't find much pleasure in staying here longer than I had to. But, it was Melissa's birthday sleepover and the arrangements for the party had already been made. This was my first sleepover and my first planned time with the girls away from the studio. I didn't really know what to expect. I mean, what could a group of lip balm applying, tutu loving, ballet girls get up to together overnight? Apparently, I was just as oblivious to the fun as Melissa's dad, who already seemed irritated upon arrival. Not to mention his reaction to the five of us waiting for him to squeeze our belongings into the car boot! It wouldn't have been as much of a challenge if the girls hadn't packed for a week! What could they have possibly loaded into their bags? Whatever it was, I was sure to find out…

A few hours into Melissa's pre-planned 'Disney movie marathon extravaganza', the girls decided that they were in the mood for a slightly more mobile activity.

Certainly inspired by Cinderella's sudden transformation for the ball, Natalie and Emma rushed toward their belongings and emptied out what seemed to be the contents of their dressing tables: lip gloss, foundation, eyeshadow trays, make up brushes. Along joined Poppy and Melissa who added to the collection, passing on the excitement like a contagious infection. Nonetheless I'd speak too soon, it seems as though I was immune! Make up was really not my thing, and not something that I would think to bring.

The girls began to organise themselves and apply makeup on each other. It was as if I entered a whole new world. Like budding artists they brushed up their faces, with lighter strokes in complex places. And concealed their freckles upon disguise, that would give them the 'glow' to highlight their eyes.

"Alison" - Emma drawing attention to the fact that I was not engaged in the activity, "Where's your make up?"

In defence I explained, "I don't have make-up and all this gear, as for this, I have no idea." The girls giggled to themselves, whilst Poppy interrupted: "Why don't you have any makeup? Every girl in school has some! Why can't you just be a normal girl? You have so far to come!" The girls all giggled again and moved closer towards me. It was like anyone who asked me this question had some sort of power over me, and regardless of how I felt, the unending need for acceptance would always override. Yet, the concept of being 'normal' seemed to always be out of reach.

"Come on girls, let's show her how it's done," Melissa directed. I didn't really want this, but I had no choice, apparently my thoughts didn't have a voice! And I was bound to lose a four V one, so within seconds this project had begun:

Natalie: "Ok, let's put on some lip gloss"

Emma: "and contour your face"

Poppy: "and draw on your eyebrows"

Melissa: "…just in case"

The girls all prepared their tools around me and took it in turns to explain and demonstrate each part of the procedure. Emma rushed into first place to make sure that I would contour my face. Though Emma's contouring didn't look like mine, because I struggled to keep within the line.

Next was Poppy with her steady hand, to draw the eyebrows and make them stand. Again, my lines would let me down, as I drew too sharp to make me frown.

Then came Natalie with her tricks, to finish off with her glossy lips. I applied it well but couldn't stand the paste, when I slipped my mouth with a taste.

Melissa then held me down and didn't release until she tidied up our masterpiece. Once she had finished the girls all circled around and watched me at the mirror with no sound.

Because in the way, spoke the words they always say: "Why can't you just be a normal girl?"

Well, if that's what you want me to be;

I'll gloss up my lips, I'll contour my face,

I'll draw on my eyebrows – if that's the case,

But really, that's NOT ME.

Girls Always Kiss Boys

The last day of term always brought me a sense of relief. Mostly, because a whole week off school meant a whole week of football! Though, also because I always managed to find an excuse to avoid the end of term school disco and make a swift exit to begin my holidays. But, of course, just like everything else that was going on in my life recently, what I really wanted and what I found myself doing were two completely different things!

As well as an obligation to attend ballet rehearsals every day of half term in preparation for our recital, I was also forced into going to the school disco by four persistent girls who wouldn't take no for an answer. Joining forces with aunt Cecilia, Natalie, Poppy, Melissa and Emma invited themselves round to get ready beforehand. Thus, with a passionate aunt eager to 'improve' my ways, four new friends to impress, and one prolonged, over-exhausted, destructive question to eliminate from my life – avoiding the disco was not an option!

So, we began to get ready and as you could probably imagine by now, there was no quick, easy, comfortable way for me to get through this. In fact, the newly imposed routine of preparing to go out managed to increase my preparation time by one whole hour! Because, as you can also imagine, my routine now consisted of dress picking, hair tidying and make up applying. As much as this new lifestyle had improved my relationships with the people around me, something still didn't feel quite right.

On our way back up to school, the girls changed their topic of conversation. Just as I thought the night couldn't get any more uncomfortable, we had to talk about boys! I didn't mind talking about boys in a sporting context, that didn't seem to bother me.

But I was uninterested in talking about them, especially in a romantic way! And just when I thought I was starting to fit in with the girls, this bombshell couldn't have launched me any further away from them! The girls all had a boy partner that they were dating or liked, and so they expressed their nerves and excitement to see them:

Poppy: "I can't wait to see James; do you think we'll kiss?"

Melissa: "I'm a little scared to see Ed, Do I look ok?"

Emma: "Ah Simon just text me, they have arrived"

Natalie: "Let's go girls, let's get our men"

One by one we entered the room and the boys approached us way too soon! The girls then stood with their 'men', there was one left over to which they had then: Yes! You know what happened here, they took a step back and moved him near. Every part of me wanted to run and knew that I should never have come!

The girls tried to give me a pep talk before they headed onto the dancefloor with their partners.

Melissa: "Come on Alison give him a chance"

Natalie: "You'll feel much better after a dance"

Poppy: "And when he leans, lean in for the kiss"

Emma: "And push out your lips so he won't miss"

As the girls walked away my arranged partner introduced himself "Hi, I'm Tom. Come on let's dance." As much as I felt bad for Tom and his efforts, I really didn't want to dance with him. And as for kissing him – Yuck!! Staying still and not replying, Tom reacted with the one thing I didn't need to hear:

"Why can't you just be a normal girl?"

I felt like a kettle waiting to boil but knowing this moment I could not spoil, I swallowed his comment that frustrated me and acted as the girl he wanted to see.

We walked over to the dancefloor and took a spot by the window. I glanced over at the girls who were so busy with their own partners, that they were in no position to help me. I mean, not that they would let me out of this situation anyway, but some form of support would have been appreciated.

With some distance I started to dance with him, and had to bite my tongue to hold within - the reply to what he would say, that angered me in every way:

"Girls always kiss boys, it's a fact. Any normal girl would know that"

He grabbed my hand and pulled me near, and every part of me wanted to veer, away from his head that began to lean but interrupted by something that I had seen:

My reflection in the window and in the way, spoke the words they always say:

"Why can't you just be a normal girl?"

Well, if that's what you want me to be;

I'll dance with the boy, I'll lean in for the kiss,

I'll push out my lips - so he won't miss,

But really, THAT'S NOT ME.

The Art of Normality

"Welcome everyone to our fifth annual ballet recital. The girls have been working extremely hard to put on this show for you…" Continues Sally, standing on stage to our audience. Waiting for our big moment, I quietly observed the girls backstage. They were a little nervous, but they were enjoying this moment and knew it was something that they wanted to be doing. I, however, still didn't feel comfortable, or that I belonged, or that I was free. Even after jumping through every hurdle to make me 'normal', I didn't feel normal and I definitely didn't feel myself.

"Let's go girls," Sally poked her head behind the curtain and the girls quickly all lined up. Every single part of me didn't want to be doing this. I was drained, emotionally drained - holding back my tears, I counted up to nine and told myself it would be fine.

We entered the stage in one long line, to the count of Sally who kept us in time. To which the music then began and for a minute I stuck to the plan. But after that, I froze still and could no longer go against my will. The performance crashed and the music stopped, and Sally's face suddenly dropped: "WHY CAN'T YOU JUST BE A NORMAL GIRL?" She said, AHH! the kettle had boiled and I saw red! The room broke into murmurs and pockets of laughter, and my frustration couldn't wait till after. All the thoughts that I had bottled in, exploded from the ache within. No longer did I even care, about laying them out and expressing them there.

I looked around the room at all the people that had asked me this question or at some point made it relevant to me by their laughs, their concerning looks and their comments. It suddenly dawned on me that the power that this question had didn't come from the question nor the people that had asked me it, but rather from the control that I allowed it to have.

And as for the term 'normal' – well, there was no such thing! There wasn't one way to be something, or do something, if there was – I wouldn't have to try and fit in, I would already be the same as every other girl. The things that made me different from everybody else were not a mistake, they were the things that made me, well; me.

In realisation, I took off the uncomfortable ugly-looking bow that I stupidly forced myself to wear and threw it with great rage on the floor. The unpredictable reaction echoed silence in the hall and addressing everyone I built up the courage to exclaim:

"Don't tell me to be normal, normal is not a thing, to think I believed the nonsense you sing. How could you create such a world, that rejects the girl who never twirled? Nor didn't like pink, boys, makeup or dolls, but playing football and scoring goals? And why is my ability to then be a contender, only defined by the terms of my gender? Yet regardless of these rules and dresses and twirls, there's more than one way to be a girl! More than one way to be human in fact, and If you didn't know, I'll tell you that: we are all different, and different is good, how happier you'd be if you understood. And if you'd break down the walls you constructed, from the parts of us that had been obstructed. You'll find some things you never knew, the things that really make us true. And when you realise that it's not strange, you'll see that it was all just a matter of change."

The room remained silent and for the first time this question and the thoughts of everyone around me, was not only irrelevant but held no significance to the way I viewed myself. I left the stage as quickly as the weight lifted off my shoulders, and unshackled my hands from the boulders, that would once keep me from running home, and getting changed to stand alone, in front of the mirror dressed as ME, to find the things that I would see:

In the way, shattered were the words they always say:
"Why can't you just be a normal girl?"
Well, I DON'T CARE what you want me to be,
I won't stop with the shorts, or tidy the 'mess',
nor wear a gown and dress to impress.
I won't stop with the football and let the boys play,
nor twirl around and do ballet.
I won't gloss up my lips or contour my face,
nor draw on my eyebrows – just in case.
I won't dance with the boy or lean in for the kiss,
nor push out my lips – so he won't miss.
BECAUSE REALLY, THAT'S JUST ME.